Soviet Union

Name	Position	Number	Name	Position	Number
Anisin, Vyacheslav	C	22	Petrov, Vladimir	C	16
Blinov, Yuri	LW	9	Ragulin, Alexander	LD	5
Bodunov, Alexander	LW	24	Shadrin, Vladimir	C	19
Gusev, Alexander	LD	2	Shatalov, Yuri	LD	14
Kharlamov, Valeri	LW	17	Solodukhin, Vyacheslav	RW	21
Kuzkin, Viktor	RD	4	Starshinov, Vyacheslav	C	8
Lebedev, Yuri	RW	23	Tretiak, Vladislav	G	20
Liapkin, Yuri	LD	25	Tsygankov, Gennady	RD	7
Lutchenko, Vladimir	LD	3	Vasiliev, Valeri	RD	6
Maltsev, Alexander	C	10	Vikulov, Vladimir	RW	18
Martynyuk, Alexander	RW	29	Volchkov, Alexander	RW	30
Mikhailov, Boris	RW	13	Yakushev, Alexander	LW	15
Mishakov, Yevgeny	LW	12	Zimin, Yevgeny	RW	11
Paladjev, Yevgeny	RD	26			

The Greatest Goal

by Mike Leonetti
illustrations by Sean Thompson

RAINCOAST BOOKS

Vancouver

First published in 2001 by

Raincoast Books
9050 Shaughnessy Street
Vancouver, British Columbia
Canada V6P 6E5
www.raincoast.com

2 3 4 5 6 7 8 9 10

National Library of Canada Cataloguing in Publication Data

Leonetti, Mike, 1958–
    The greatest goal

    ISBN 1-55192-318-1 (bound). — ISBN 1-55192-574-5 (pbk.)

    1. Canada-U.S.S.R. Hockey Series, 1972—Juvenile literature.
I. Thompson, Sean, 1966– II. Title.
GV847.25.L46 2001   J796.962´66   C2001-910860-5

Edited by Scott Steedman
Designed by Val Speidel

Acknowledgements
The writer would like to thank the staff at Raincoast for being very encouraging in developing this story. The assistance of Rachelle Kanefsky was very valuable in refining the story. A very heartfelt thanks to Sean Thompson whose artistic talents are simply incredible and make this book all the more special. I would like to thank my wife, Maria, for her help in providing me with valuable feedback, and my son, David, for giving me the inspiration to write books for young kids. I would also like to give a special thank you to Paul Henderson for scoring the goal no one will ever forget and for giving an unknown writer a chance when I asked him if I could write his autobiography. A big cheer to all the members of Team Canada 1972!

Printed and bound in Singapore

This book is dedicated to all Canadians who watched or
listened to the game on September 28, 1972,
and to a new generation that wants to know why
this moment was so special for Canada.
– ML

To my wife, Rachelle, for her love and support,
and to the miracles performed down at the local rink.
– ST

It was a warm Saturday morning in early September. The leaves were just starting to change colour. Fall was right around the corner … and so was the start of the hockey season.

Dad and I were playing ball hockey on the driveway just like we tried to do every day after he got home from work. Dad was in goal and I was taking shots. I imagined I was Paul Henderson of the Toronto Maple Leafs. I faked to the left and then unleashed my wrist shot. Goal! Dad had gone down early.

Dad looked up and said, "Wow Paul, that shot should get you some goals this season."

My dad had taught me to skate. He had played in leagues since he was a kid. Now I was in a league too. Next Saturday we wouldn't be playing ball hockey in the driveway. We would be at the rink for my first game of the season!

Today was special for another reason. The biggest hockey series of all time started tonight: Canada versus the Soviet Union. For the first time ever, the best Canadian NHL players would play against the best players from the Soviet Union in an eight-game series.

I took control of the ball again. Dad liked to imagine he was Ken Dryden of the Montreal Canadiens when he was in goal. I wheeled and unleashed a blistering slapshot. **Save!**

"Do you think Canada will win all eight games, Dad?"

"I don't know if we'll win all eight," Dad said. "But with our players we should win the series without too much trouble. I'm so excited! What a way to start the hockey season!"

"I hope Paul Henderson has a great series," I said as I wove with the ball in front of the net. I never missed watching Henderson every Saturday night on *Hockey Night in Canada*. My friends admired players like Frank Mahovlich and Phil Esposito, but I liked Henderson best because he skated really fast and scored lots of goals—just this past season, he had scored 38! My Mom liked him because he always protected his head when he played, and she bought me a helmet just like his. He also had the same first name as me, Paul.

Dad tried a poke check, but I pulled the ball back and beat him with a backhand shot. He scOres!

That night Dad and I were tucked in on the couch to watch the start of the Canada-Soviet series. The first game was in Montreal and the fans gave the biggest cheer to the Montreal Canadien players on Team Canada as they were introduced. I watched closely as Paul Henderson skated out. The look on his face seemed to say he was ready to play.

When the national anthem was played, the fans sung along loudly. Then Prime Minister Trudeau dropped the puck, and finally we were ready to plAy hockey!

When the game started, Phil Esposito scored after just 30 seconds of play! My dad and I let out a cheer, and before I knew it, Henderson scored to make it 2-0. He snapped in a shot from a face-off so quickly, the Russian goalie had no chance.

"You're right, Dad, our best are too gOod for them," I said.

But then things started to change—quickly. The Russians got two fast goals to tie the score, and by the end of the second period they were up 4-2. Bobby Clarke got a goal back in the third but the Canadians were looking tired.

The Russian players were buzzing around, creating chance after chance. They scored three more times and won the game 7-3. The Soviet goalie, Vladislav Tretiak, was blocking more shots than anyone had ever imagined. He wore a strange mask that looked like a bird cage and he had a great glove hand. My dad and I couldn't beliEve what had happened!

Two days later, the second game was played in Toronto. Could Team Canada come back to tie the series? I was excited about watching the game with Dad, but he couldn't be at home that night. He had been promoted in his job and now he had to travel for work. It was hard to get used to him being away, especially for one of the biggest hockey games of all time.

I watched the game on my own and saw Canada win 4-1. It was really close, and Team Canada had a slim 2-1 lead when they got a penalty in the third period. Then Peter Mahovlich scored an amAzing short-handed goal when he took the puck down the ice and fooled a Russian defenceman with a great fake before deking Tretiak out of position. The crowd at Maple Leaf Gardens went cRazy. The Canadian players poured on to the ice to congratulate Mahovlich. "That's more like it," I said, but then I remembered that Dad wasn't there to hear me.

The next day was the start of the school year, so I was up early for breakfast. I told Dad all about the game the night before. "I sure missed watching it with you," I said.

"I try to be with you whenever I can, Paul, but sometimes I need to get things done for my job. I'm just like the players on Team Canada. I try my best but it doesn't always work out the way I would like."

"Can we watch the next game together?"

"I hope so."

I loved the start of school because it meant seeing all of my friends again after a long summer. This year all we talked about was hockey. I was in Grade Four and my teacher, Mr. McGettigan, let me do my first class project on the series.

Flin Flon

Vancouver
Game 4

Regina

Winnipeg
Game 3

I learned about Montreal, Toronto, Winnipeg and Vancouver, the cities where the four Canadian games were being played. I also learned that a lot of the Canadian players came from small towns like mine.

Yvan Cournoyer was from Drummondville, Quebec; Henderson was born in Kincardine, Ontario; Bobby Clarke grew up in Flin Flon, Manitoba; and Red Berenson was from Regina, Saskatchewan. Some other great players on the team were Serge Savard, Guy Lapointe, Brad Park, Rod Gilbert, Jean Ratelle and brothers Phil and Tony Esposito.

So many great NHL players from all over the country had come together to create one of the best teams ever!

Montreal
Game 1

Drummondville

Toronto
Game 2

Kincardine

The third game took place in Winnipeg. From the start, Dad and I were in position on the couch. Canada scored an early goal but the Russians quickly tied it up. We got two more, and the Russians added a second. Then Henderson raced in to pick up a loose puck just over the blue line and sLapped it past Tretiak to make it 4-2 for Canada.

But before the end of the second period, the Russians had scored another two and evened the score. Henderson had a great chance to win the game in the third period when he was right in front of the net. He put his arms in the air for just a second, thinking he had scored, but Tretiak made a spectAcular save. The horn sounded, signalling the end of the game. The Soviets and Canada had tied 4-4.

"Well, Paul," my dad said, "I guess you should never count on a game being won before it's over. Those Soviets are tough."

I was allowed to stay up a little later than usual to watch the fourth game, which was played in Vancouver. But Canada lost 5-3, and our team was boOed by the crowd.

After the game, Phil Esposito, one of the captains of the team, made a speech while he was being interviewed on television.

"To the people across Canada—we're tryiNg our bEst," he said. "Every one of us, we came out and played for Team Canada because we love our country and not for any other reason. I don't think it's fair that we should be booed."

Mr. McGettigan had handed out postcards at school. Each one had a Canadian flag on the front with the words "Go Canada!" I thought what Esposito had said was really fantaStic, so I decided to write my postcard to Paul Henderson to inspire him.

"Good luck in the rest of the series and I hope you score some goals!" was the message I wrote.

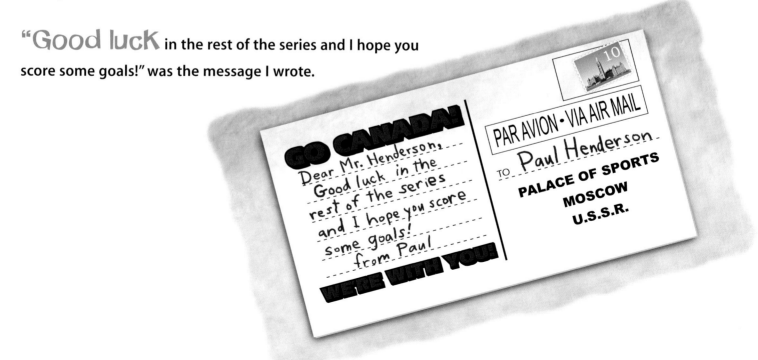

GO CANADA!

Dear Mr. Henderson,
Good luck in the rest of the series and I hope you score some goals!
from Paul

WE'RE WITH YOU!

PAR AVION · VIA AIR MAIL
TO Paul Henderson
PALACE OF SPORTS
MOSCOW
U.S.S.R.

10

Dad was away for the week on a business trip. I missed having him home, especially since I was about to start to play in my league on Saturday. Mom took me to the game and my baby sister Danielle came along as well. It was great having them in the stands watching me. But during the game, my coach got upSet at me because he said I didn't pass the puck enough. My Dad had told me I would become a better player if I handled the puck more.

I really trIEd to make good passes whenever I could, but I loved to carry the puck up the ice and stickhandle my way around the other team.

I told Mom what had happened. She was very good about listening to me but I still wished I could talk to Dad about this because it was a hockey problem. He had a way of explaining things to me about the game. I was trying to play the way he taught me.

The next few days went by slowly. Both the Canadian and the Soviet teams were travelling to Moscow for the fifth game of the series. We had to win a game. We just Had to!

Because of the time difference, the games in Moscow would be played in the afternoon. At school, all us kids were going crazy at the thought of missing Game Five. Suddenly the principal, Mr. Melady, announced over the loudspeaker, "All staff and students report to the cafeteria. We have a game to watch!" A huGe cheer went up throughout the school.

The game looked very different inside the Russian arena. The ice surface was so much larger. There were 3,000 Canadian fans who had gone to Moscow and you could hear them cheering. It must have helped because Team Canada jumped to a 3-1 lead! Henderson scored one of the goals. Then in the third period, he used his blazing speed to break away from everyone on the ice. He moved in on the Russian net and fired a hot shot past Tretiak!

But then the Soviets scored four goals in six minutes to win the game 5-4. It couldn't possibly get any worse! Canada was about to lose the whole series. All the Soviets needed was one more win.

Later that day I had hockey practice. Mom picked me up when it was over because Dad was still at work. She could see that I was sad.

"It's not so bad, Paul," Mom said. "There's a chance Team Canada can come back and win."

"I don't think so, Mom," I said quietly. "They'd have to win three games in a row, and all the Soviets have to do is win one."

"Now Paul, don't you lose hope …," Mom tried to reassure me.

"Is Dad going to be home tonight?" I asked.

"He's working late, but he should be home before bedtime. It's really busy at work right now," she said.

"I know, I just wanted to talk to him, that's all."

I could tell Mom wanted to talk some more, but I was so sad, all I could do was shrug and look away.

Then, just when it looked like things would never improve for Canada, everything started to change. The sixth game was played on a Sunday afternoon. Dad was working in his study, but he promised he would come out into the living room and check on the score. Team Canada just had to win … and they did, with a 3-2 victory. Best of all, **HeNderson** scored the winning goal.

The seventh game was even more exciting. Mr. McGettigan brought a television into our classroom for the third period. The score was tied 3-3 with just over two minutes left to play when my hero Henderson came through again. He took a pass from Serge Savard just over centre ice and broke in on two Soviet defencemen. He somehow managed to get by both of them, and then, just as he was falling, snapped a shot over Tretiak's shoulder. It was one of the bEst goals I'd ever seen!

Canada had won the game 4-3 and evened the series. It was all down to the final game!

After the bell rang at the end of the day, my friends and I played ball hockey in the schoolyard. We all pretended to be Canadian players. Team Canada suddenly had a chance to win the series. I thought how happy my Dad would be if we won. It was too bad we couldn't watch the game together. Dad would be at work and I would be at school.

On Thursday, Mr. McGettigan brought a television into our classroom for the final game. It started badly for Canada, and the Soviets finished the second period with a 5-3 lead. It looked like all of Team Canada's efforts would be wasted!

Just then, Principal Melady announced that we could watch the end of the game at home if we wanted to. It was fun being with all my friends, but there was nothing like watching hockey in my very own house, especially since we had just bought a colour TV! I bOlted for the door and ran all the way home.

When I rushed into the house I found Mom and Danielle in front of the TV and … I could hardly believe it: Dad was there too! He had left work early to watch the big game.

"Hey there, what are you doing home?" Dad asked with a big smile. "Jump up here on the couch."

The third period was just beginning. Phil Esposito, who was playing with great heart and determination, scored early to make it 5-4. Before I knew it, Cournoyer scored to make it 5-5, and we all let out a scReam. There were still over seven minutes left to play!

"This should be an exciting finish!" Dad said.

Both teams were playing very cautiously, not wanting to make a mistake. It was so tense! But the players were tired and the game was quickly coming to an end. There would be no overtime. It looked like the whole series would end in a tie. I could barely sit still!

Then, in the final minute, Henderson came darting across the ice. We all began cheering, "Go HenderSon Go!"

Suddenly, my hero was in front of the Soviet net. Esposito whacked a shot off the goalie. The puck came right to Henderson. He swatted it at the net, but Tretiak stopped the shot. The rebound came back to Henderson and he put the puck right into the net!

The announcer yelled out, "Henderson has scored for Canada!" Dad and I jumped up and hugged, screaming, "We scored! We scored!" Team Canada was up 6-5 with only 34 seconds left to play. Canada was going to win the greatest hockey series ever played!

As soon as the game was over, Dad, Mom, Danielle and I went outside to join our neighbours on the street. Everyone was out celebrating. Dad put me on his shoulders so that I could see what was going on. Someone was playing "O Canada" on a trumpet and kids were running up and down the street with a big Canadian flag. We were all so hAppy!

Saturday morning I woke up early and found Dad ready and waiting to take me to my hockey game. In the car I asked him, "Dad, you say stickhandling is important, but the coach keeps telling me to pass to the open man …?"

"We're both right, Paul. It's important to have good puck skills, but hockey's a team sport and the open man has the best chance. Besides, you'll be surprised how often you get the puck back when you pass it."

I could hear Dad encouraging my team during the game. Then I broke up a play and passed the puck to our winger as he broke down the ice. I took off after him. He hammered a hard shot as he crossed the blue line. The goalie made the save, but the rebound came straight to me and I fired it home. **GOAL!** My dad cheered from the stands. As we walked back to the car afterwards we talked about how I had played, just like we always did.

Dad patted me on the shoulder and said, "You know Paul, watching that final game together reminded me how much fun we have because of hockey."
"Of course, Dad," I said. "But I know you have to work, too."
"Work is important Paul, but so are you, Danielle and your mom. And I don't want to miss any of your hockey games." He faked to the left and took an imaginary shot. "Do you think you'll score next Saturday?"

I just smiled. I knew I would never forget that I was with my biggest hero, my dad, the day that my hockey hero, Paul Henderson, scored the greatest goal.

Paul Henderson

Paul Henderson began his professional hockey career with the Detroit Red Wings in 1963. He was traded to the Toronto Maple Leafs in 1968, and played with them until 1974. He then signed with the Toronto Toros of the World Hockey Association (WHA). In 1976, the Toros became the Birmingham Bulls, and Henderson played for them until 1979. He was back in the NHL with the Atlanta Flames in 1979-80, his last of 18 pro hockey seasons. In 707 NHL games, Henderson scored 236 goals and added 241 assists. In the WHA, he netted 140 goals and 143 assists in 360 games.

During the 1972 Canada-Soviet series, Henderson played on a line with Ron Ellis, a fellow Leaf, and Bobby Clarke. He finished with 7 goals and a total of 10 points in eight games. His last three goals were all game-winners, and his final goal in Game Eight, scored with only 34 seconds left to play, will forever be remembered as "The Goal."

The fame of scoring such a memorable goal caused Henderson to re-examine his life and make significant changes. Since his retirement from hockey, he has run a Christian ministry that concentrates on helping men become better husbands and fathers. Wherever he goes, people still tell Henderson stories about what they were doing the moment the goal was scored. One of those stories was the inspiration for this book.

About the 1972 Canada-Soviet Series

For many years, only amateur teams had been allowed to play against the Russians. All that changed in 1972, when, for the first time ever, the best Canadian professional hockey players got a chance to play the best of the Soviet Union. Canadian fans looked forward to the series with great anticipation. Many commentators believed that the professionals would destroy the so-called "amateurs." It did not turn out that way and the Canadian team had to show great heart and determination to take the eight-game series 4-3-1.

The original group selected to play for Team Canada consisted of 35 professionals, all from NHL teams. Fifteen of these players would one day be elected to the Hockey Hall of Fame. Some of the other outstanding Canadian players not mentioned in this story were Ron Ellis, Gary Bergman, Dennis Hull, Bill White, Pat Stapleton and J. P. Parise. The best Soviet players in the series included Alexander Yakushev (11 points), Vladimir Shadrin (8 points), Valeri Kharlamov (7 points), Vladimir Petrov (7 points) and Hall of Fame goaltender Vladislav Tretiak, who played in all eight games.

About the Soviet Union

The Soviet Union was officially formed in 1922, after the Russian Revolution and a long civil war. It was made up of Russia plus 14 other Communist republics. A massive country spanning two continents—Asia and Europe—the Soviet Union took up nearly one sixth of the world's land surface. After World War II, it became the main rival of the Western countries—the United States, Canada and Western Europe—with their different political, social and economic systems. This "Cold War" lasted until 1991, when Communism was officially abandoned and the Soviet Union broke down into different countries. These new countries are trying to develop democratic governments like those in the West.

Final Scores

GAME 1	Sept. 2, 1972, Montreal. Soviet Union 7 – Team Canada 3.
GAME 2	Sept. 4, 1972, Toronto. Team Canada 4 – Soviet Union 1.
GAME 3	Sept. 6, 1972, Winnipeg. Team Canada 4 – Soviet Union 4.
GAME 4	Sept. 8, 1972, Vancouver. Soviet Union 5 – Team Canada 3.
GAME 5	Sept. 22, 1972, Moscow. Soviet Union 5 – Team Canada 4.
GAME 6	Sept. 24, 1972, Moscow. Team Canada 3 – Soviet Union 2.
GAME 7	Sept. 26, 1972, Moscow. Team Canada 4 – Soviet Union 3.
GAME 8	Sept. 28, 1972, Moscow. Team Canada 6 – Soviet Union 5.

Team Canada

Name	Position	Number	Name	Position	Number
Awrey, Don	RD	26	Johnston, Ed	G	1
Berenson, Red	C	15	Lapointe, Guy	LD	25
Bergman, Gary	LD	2	Mahovlich, Frank	LW	27
Cashman, Wayne	LW	14	Mahovlich, Pete	LW	20
Clarke, Bobby	C	28	Martin, Richard	LW	36
Cournoyer, Yvan	RW	12	Mikita, Stan	C	21
Dionne, Marcel	C	34	Orr, Bobby	D	4
Dryden, Ken	G	29	Parise, Jean-Paul	LW	22
Ellis, Ron	RW	6	Park, Brad	RD	5
Esposito, Phil	C	7	Perreault, Gilbert	C	33
Esposito, Tony	G	35	Ratelle, Jean	C	18
Gilbert, Rod	RW	8	Redmond, Mickey	RW	24
Glennie, Brian	D	38	Savard, Serge	RD	23
Goldsworthy, Bill	RW	9	Seiling, Rod	LD	16
Guevremont, Jocelyn	D	37	Tallon, Dale	D	32
Hadfield, Vic	LW	11	Stapleton, Pat	LD	3
Henderson, Paul	LW	19	White, Bill	RD	17
Hull, Dennis	LW	10			